Little Bird
and the
Moon Sandwich

Linda Berkowitz

Crown Publishers, Inc. New York

For my son, David Wikler

CROWN is a trademark of Crown Publishers, Inc. Printed in Singapore

Library of Congress Cataloging-in-Publication Data: Berkowitz, Linda. Little Bird and the moon sandwich / Linda Berkowitz.   p.   cm.
Summary: When they see the moon in the water, Little Bird, Alfonse, and the other geese dive to the bottom of the pond in an attempt to retrieve it.
[1. Birds—Fiction. 2. Geese—Fiction. 3. Moon—Fiction.] I. Title.
PZ7.W6415Li   1998
[E]–dc21   97-24270

ISBN 0-517-70961-9 (trade) — 0-517-70962-7 (lib. bdg.) 10 9 8 7 6 5 4 3 2 1 First Edition

123070

"It's dark and blue," peeped Little Bird.

"And I see the moon," honked Alfonse.

"I want to touch it!" peeped Little Bird.

"You can't touch the moon!" Alfonse honked. "It's too high up."

"If it fell, could I touch it?" asked Little Bird.

"No," said Alfonse, "the moon can't fall because it is glued onto the sky. Also, the moon is made of Swiss cheese."

"Oh," Little Bird sighed. "If the moon did fall, I would make a moon sandwich, and it would taste good!"

They walked a little farther
and the moon disappeared.

"Where could it be?" Alfonse honked.

"There it is!" Little Bird peeped. "It fell in the water, and I am going to get it," she said,

and she jumped in.

"Me first!" Alfonse honked,
and he jumped in.

Along came the other geese.

"What are you doing?" they asked.

"The moon fell in the water," said Little Bird, "and I am going to get it."

The geese looked in the water.

"I see it!" honked a big white goose. "It's mine!"

"Mine!" honked another. Soon all the geese were in the water, splashing and honking, honking and splashing, and making a racket!

A white goose dove to the bottom and came up with something in her bill. "Here it is," she honked. "Here is the moon!"

"That is not fair!" peeped Little Bird. "I saw the moon *first!*"

"That is not the moon," honked Alfonse. "That is a rock!"

"Oh," honked the geese. Then they splashed and honked, and honked and splashed some more. Another goose dove down to the bottom and came up with something in his bill.

"I found it!" he said. "Here is the moon!"
"It is round," honked the geese.
"It is yellow," peeped Little Bird.
"That is not the moon!" said Alfonse.
"That is a tennis ball!"

So ... the geese splashed and honked, and honked and splashed again.
Another goose dove down to the bottom and came up with something
in her bill.

"Here it is," she said. "Here is the moon!"
"That is not the moon," said Alfonse. "That is a Swiss cheese sandwich."

"Let me see! Let me see!" cried Little Bird.
Alfonse and the other geese were hungry. They honked
and splashed, and splashed and honked, and ate it all up!

"The geese ate my moon sandwich!"
Little Bird peeped sadly.
   "Don't be sad, Little Bird," said Alfonse.
"I saved you a piece."
   "Oh. Thank you very much!" peeped
Little Bird. "You are a nice goose."

Little Bird took her piece of moon
sandwich and looked at it lovingly. She
did *not* eat it.

"I knew you weren't glued onto the
sky," she said to it.

Later, Alfonse told her, "The moon isn't really made of Swiss cheese."

"Oh!" said Little Bird. "I knew that."

"Is the moon really a big light shining on me in the darkness?" Little Bird asked.

"Yes," answered Alfonse. "How did you know that?"

"Zzzzzz," snored Little Bird.